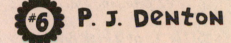

#6 **P. J. Denton**

Grab your pillow and join the

P. J. DENTON

Sleepover Squad

#6 The New Girl

Illustrated by Julia Denos

ALADDIN PAPERBACKS

NEW YORK   LONDON   TORONTO   SYDNEY

This book is a work of fiction. Any references to historical events, real people, or real locales are used fictitiously. Other names, characters, places, and incidents are the product of the author's imagination, and any resemblance to actual events or locales or persons, living or dead, is entirely coincidental.

ALADDIN PAPERBACKS

An imprint of Simon & Schuster Children's Publishing Division

1230 Avenue of the Americas, New York, NY 10020

Text copyright © 2008 by Catherine Hapka

Illustrations copyright © 2008 by Julia Denos

All rights reserved, including the right of reproduction in whole or in part in any form.

ALADDIN PAPERBACKS, series name and logo, and colophon are trademarks of Simon & Schuster, Inc.

Designed by Karin Paprocki

The text of this book was set in Cochin.

Manufactured in the United States of America

First Aladdin Paperbacks edition October 2008

2 4 6 8 10 9 7 5 3

Library of Congress Control Number 2007943608

ISBN-13: 978-1-4169-5932-8

ISBN-10: 1-4169-5932-7

* 1 *

Autumn Is Awesome!

What do you guys think?" Jo Sanchez asked.

She had just finished drawing and coloring in a bunch of maple and oak leaves. Now she held up the paper so her three best friends—Emily McDougal, Kara Wyatt, and Taylor Kent—could see it. The four of them were sharing one of the big, wooden-topped tables in the sunny art room at Oak Tree

Elementary School. Today's class project was to create pictures of autumn leaves like the ones decorating the trees outside. Emily was the first one to look up.

"That looks really good, Jo," she said in her soft voice. "Your maple leaves are the same shade of red as the real ones on the tree outside my bedroom window."

"Thanks, Emily." Jo smiled at her friend. Emily was good at art. She also knew a lot about trees, since she and her parents lived on a small farm with lots of trees on it. Besides that, she was super honest. If she said that Jo's leaf picture looked realistic, she meant it.

That made Jo happy. She wasn't as good at art as Emily, but she liked to get things right—especially when it came to school. She was one of the best students in the third grade.

Jo looked over at her other two best friends. It looked as though neither of them had heard her question. Kara's springy red hair was falling over her freckled face as she bent over her own leaf picture. She was concentrating so hard that her tongue was sticking out of the corner of her mouth.

"Rats!" Kara cried out suddenly. She tossed away the orange crayon she had been using. "I went outside the lines again!"

"Never mind, Kara," Emily said, tucking her long, pale blond hair behind her ear. "That just makes it more artistic. Lots of famous artists do stuff like go outside the lines."

Jo smiled. Emily was good at coming up with the nicest possible way to tell the truth.

Just then Jessica Polk skipped past on her way to the pencil sharpener. She glanced down at everyone's drawings as she passed their table. That was no surprise. Jessica was the class busybody. She liked to know everything that was going on with everyone all the time. "Hey, Taylor!" Jessica blurted out in her loud voice. "You're supposed to be drawing leaves, not soccer balls!"

Jo grinned and leaned over to look at Taylor's picture. There was part of a leaf drawn in the middle of the paper. But all around the edges were sketches of soccer balls, soccer goals, and even a pair of soccer cleats. The drawings were kind of sloppy. Taylor was very smart and got pretty good grades in most subjects as long as she remembered to pay attention. But she was a little too impatient to be good at drawing.

Taylor finally looked up from her paper. "Oops," she said. "I guess I got distracted thinking about my soccer tournament. I can hardly believe it's less than a week away!"

The boys sitting at the next art table had heard Jessica's loud comment. Randy Blevins jumped out of his seat and ran over to peek at Taylor's drawing.

"Check it out," he called back to his friends. "I think Taylor must've got brain damage from heading her stupid soccer balls too hard. She thinks soccer balls grow on trees!"

His friend Max Wolfe laughed loudly. He ran over to look for himself. "No way, that's not it, you dummy!" he cried. "Taylor's just obsessed with sports, that's all. She probably forgot she's supposed to be a girl." He pointed to Taylor's short, curly black hair. "See? She even has a boy's haircut!"

Jo rolled her eyes. "Is that your idea of a joke, Max?" she asked. "Because it's not funny. It doesn't even make sense. A lot of girls have short hair, and a lot like sports just as much as boys do."

Taylor grinned. "You tell them, Jo-Jo," she said. "I definitely know I'm not a boy. See, I know how to use my brain for something other than keeping my ears apart."

"Yeah!" Kara exclaimed loudly. "So shut up, you brainless boys!"

Jo noticed that Emily was shooting nervous looks toward the art teacher, Mr. Lutz, who was bent over his desk at the front of the room. Emily always got nervous when people argued or were too loud. She also hated getting in trouble, and most teachers didn't like it when students talked too loudly or got out of their seats. Jo didn't like getting in trouble either, but she wasn't too worried. Mr. Lutz wasn't like most teachers.

Finally Mr. Lutz looked up from his work. "What's all the commotion over there, kiddos?" he asked.

Mr. Lutz was big and tall, with bright blue eyes, little, round, wire-rimmed glasses, and a reddish-brown beard that covered most of his face. His voice was sort of rumbly and he had a Southern accent. Emily said when Mr. Lutz talked it sounded like a tree singing. That was the kind of thing only Emily would say.

Jo thought it sounded kind of cool, even though it didn't really make sense.

"I told you guys you could talk while you created," the art teacher went on. "But I didn't say that you could hold philosophical debates at the top of your lungs while running around the room." He winked and smiled. "What do you all think this is, gym class?"

"Sorry, Mr. Lutz." Randy waited until the teacher looked down again. Then he stuck out his tongue at the girls and scurried back to his own table.

"Never mind those stupid boys, Taylor." Kara shot Randy and his friends one last glare. Then she looked at Taylor's picture, and her face brightened. "Hey, that reminds me. Did you guys ask your parents about the sleepover?"

Jo nodded eagerly along with the others. She and her three best friends had their own special club called the

Sleepover Squad. They held sleepovers as often as they could. It was time for another one, and Kara wanted to have it at her house. They had decided to hold it on the day after Thanksgiving, which was less than two weeks away.

"My parents said yes," Jo said. "But, wait—why did Taylor's picture remind you of the sleepover, Kara?"

Jo was a very logical person. It bugged her when things didn't make sense. And it didn't make much sense that Taylor's drawing had reminded Kara of the sleepover. Then again, Jo knew that Kara's mind wasn't as logical as her own. Sometimes she didn't seem to make any sense at all!

"Well, it was going to be a surprise. But you guys know I'm terrible at surprises." Kara giggled. "So I'll just tell you now. I thought this sleepover would be a great time to celebrate Taylor's awesome soccer season. That can be our party theme!"

"Wow, that's so cool, K!" Taylor's greenish-gold eyes shone. "But I thought since the sleepover is the day after Thanksgiving, that would be the theme."

"Why can't we do both?" Emily asked. "Nobody ever said a sleepover can only have *one* theme."

Kara giggled again. "Yeah," she agreed. "Besides, if Taylor's team wins the big game, she'll definitely be thankful for that, right?"

Jo smiled. "That makes perfect sense to me."

Jo was still thinking about the sleepover when she got off the bus that afternoon. She hurried into her house, shivering in her light jacket. It was getting dark earlier every day. As soon as the sun started to go down, the air got crisp and chilly.

Inside, she found her mother sitting at the computer in her home office. "Guess what, Mom," Jo said. "We have a double theme for our next sleepover. It's going to be Thanksgiving *and* Taylor's soccer tournament."

"That's nice, Jo." Mrs. Sanchez looked up from the computer. "I have some news for you, too."

Jo was very observant, even when she was excited about something. Now she noticed that her mother looked kind of excited, too.

"What is it?" she asked curiously.

Her mother smiled. "Your cousin Ceci is coming to visit," she said. "She'll be arriving on Saturday afternoon, and staying right through Thanksgiving weekend!"

Exciting News

R eally? Ceci's coming here?" Jo exclaimed. "Oh my gosh, that's awesome!"

Ceci was the same age as Jo. Her father and Jo's mother were brother and sister, which made the two girls cousins. Ceci's family lived far away, in California, so she and Jo hardly ever got to see each other in person. But they kept in touch through letters, e-mails, and phone calls.

Mrs. Sanchez nodded. "Aunt Lena and Uncle Miguel have to take an important business trip overseas," she explained. "So they decided Ceci could fly out and spend Thanksgiving week with us."

"This is going to be so cool!" Jo danced around the office with excitement. "I can't wait till Ceci gets here. First I want her to meet my friends, and then I'll show her my school and the park and the tennis courts and the rest of town, and after that maybe we can go to the movies and skating and . . ."

Her mother chuckled. "All that sounds fun," she said. "But for right now, I need you to set the table for dinner. Your father should be home any minute."

"Okay." Jo danced out of the den and down the hall to the kitchen, thinking about Ceci's visit. Next week had seemed exciting enough before. There was Taylor's big championship game to look forward to, then Thanksgiving, and finally the sleepover.

And now that Ceci was coming, Jo was sure it was going to be the best week ever!

The next morning Jo ran from the bus to the front door of the school. Then she slowed to a very fast walk. Running wasn't allowed in the halls. But she wanted to share her news with her best friends as soon as possible.

She found them standing in their usual spot outside the classroom door. "I'm glad you guys are all here," she said breathlessly. "Guess what?"

"No, *you* guess what first!" Kara blurted out, her hazel eyes dancing with excitement. "My mom is getting us a cake from the bakery decorated like a soccer ball! Isn't that cool?" She licked her lips, looking hungry. "I hope she hides it so my brothers can't eat it before the sleepover even starts."

Taylor was holding a real soccer ball. She bounced it off her knee and caught it again.

"I just hope we win the big game on Sunday," she said. "Our team was terrible at practice yesterday."

"Don't worry, Taylor," Emily spoke up. "I think there's a rule about that. If you have a terrible practice before an important game, it means the game will definitely go great. It works for plays and stuff too."

"Thanks, Emmers." Taylor grinned. "I hope you're right about that. Because I want to kick that other team's butts on Sunday!"

"Guys . . . ," Jo tried, still eager to tell them about Ceci's visit.

But they hardly seemed to notice she was there. "Do you think your brothers will try to play any pranks on us this time?" Taylor asked Kara, bouncing the ball off her knee again. "Remember all the practical jokes they pulled last time we had a sleepover at your house?"

"Ugh! Don't remind me." Kara rolled her eyes. She had four brothers who loved to play jokes on everyone, especially her. "They'd better not try anything like that again. I was ready to stuff them all down the toilet that time. And if I clogged up the toilet, Mom and Dad probably wouldn't let me have any more sleepovers."

Emily and Taylor laughed. "Good point," Taylor said. "Maybe you should lock them in a closet instead."

"Guys!" Jo put in a little louder. "Listen, I have something to tell you."

"In a second, Jo-Jo." Taylor danced in place, flipping the soccer ball from one knee to the other. She laughed when it flew off to the side and bounced off a locker. "Score!" she cried, darting forward to scoop it up. "But listen, Kara, maybe we should plan a few pranks of our own, just in case. What do you think?"

Emily looked worried. She wasn't a big fan of practical jokes. "Are you sure that's a good idea?" she asked.

"Totally," Taylor said. "It worked last time, right? Kara's brothers were really surprised when we —"

"Hey, you guys!" Jo shouted at the top of her lungs.

That made all three of her friends shut up right away. They turned toward her, looking surprised.

"What's the matter, Jo-Jo?" Taylor asked.

Jo took a deep breath. "Nothing," she said. "But I have big news, and I can't wait any longer to tell you, and you guys won't stop talking!"

"Oops!" Kara giggled. "Sorry about that, Jo. What's the news?"

Jo smiled. "Ceci is coming to stay with us for a whole week!" she announced.

For a second, Taylor and Kara looked confused. But Emily nodded. "That's your cousin who lives in California, right?" she asked.

"Right," Jo said. "My family has visited

Ceci's house in California a couple of times. But she's never been here — at least not since we were babies." She giggled. "I don't really remember that far back. And Ceci probably doesn't either. So this place will seem all new to her!"

"Oh!" Now Taylor didn't look confused anymore. "I remember now. You've talked about Ceci before. She sounds cool."

"She is," Jo said. "She's the best. She's really smart and funny, and she isn't afraid to try anything. One time back in first grade when I was visiting her, she dared me to pick up this little lizard we found in her yard and put it on my head. She found another one, and we walked in and sat down for dinner wearing lizards for hats."

Kara giggled. "That's funny. I can't wait to meet her."

"Don't worry, you'll get your chance this Saturday." Jo shivered with excitement as she realized that Saturday was only a few days away. She could hardly wait!

For the rest of the week, Jo kept remembering more fun things she and Ceci had done together and more  funny things Ceci had said. She interrupted a lunchtime conversation about the sleepover to tell her friends about going with Ceci to the big theme park near her house in California. She broke into a discussion of Taylor's soccer tournament to explain that Ceci's name was short for Cecilia—Cecilia Marie Torres was her whole name, to be exact. On Friday after school, she even called Kara on the phone to tell her how good Ceci was at swimming and diving.

Kara giggled. "I don't even need to meet Ceci tomorrow," she said. "You've already told us everything there is to know about her. Since when did you turn into such a blabbermouth, Jo?"

Jo grinned. She knew that Kara was only joking. "Sorry," she said. "I guess I have been talking about her a lot. But you guys will see why I'm so excited when you meet her. Ceci is the best!"

✳ 3 ✳

Hola Ceci

Jo checked her watch for the millionth time. "When is Ceci's plane going to get here?" she said with a sigh. "I can't believe it's so late!"

Her father looked up from his newspaper. "It happens, *mi cara*," he said. "I'm sure she'll be here soon. Just try to be patient."

Normally Jo was a pretty patient person, especially compared to Kara or Taylor. But today she could hardly stand

to wait another second for the plane to arrive. It seemed as if she'd already been waiting forever!

Besides, she knew that all her friends were at Kara's house at that very moment waiting for her to get there so they could meet Ceci and finish planning next weekend's sleepover. It was the only time they could do it, since Taylor had been at soccer practice all morning getting ready for her big game the following day. Jo had convinced her parents to stop off at Kara's house on their way home from the airport.

Jo's mother was sitting next to her husband. She checked her watch.

"Maybe you should call your friends, Jo," she said. "I don't think we'll have time to drop in at Kara's house after all."

"What?" Jo's heart sank. "But my friends are dying to meet Ceci right away!"

Her father pulled his cell phone out of his pocket. "Such is life, *mi cara*," he said. "They'll just have to try to stay alive until tomorrow and meet her then."

Jo sighed, taking the phone from him. There was no point in arguing. She knew her parents were right. By the time the plane got there and they drove all the way back to town, her friends would have gone home for dinner.

Kara answered the phone on the first

ring. "Jo, is that you?" she exclaimed without even saying hello first.

Even though she was feeling impatient and disappointed, Jo couldn't help laughing. "What would you say if it wasn't me?" she asked.

Kara giggled. "I'd probably pretend it was a wrong number. Especially if it was someone calling for one of my brothers. But never mind that. Where are you guys?"

"Still at the airport." Jo explained that the plane had been delayed and still wasn't there yet. "So I guess we won't have time to make it to your house today."

"Aw, man!" Kara exclaimed. "It already feels weird planning the sleepover without you."

"Don't worry. I know you guys will do a good job." Jo bit her lip. "I just wish you didn't have to wait even longer to meet Ceci."

"That's okay. We'll be able to meet her tomorrow afternoon at Taylor's soccer game."

"Yeah. See you then."

Jo hung up and handed the phone back to her father. Then she sat down on one of the hard plastic airport chairs and tapped her fingers on the knees of her jeans. She tried to think of something to do to distract herself from being impatient. She decided to count backward from one thousand. If Ceci's plane hadn't arrived by the time she got to one, she wasn't sure what she would do. Maybe she would stomp around and yell like Taylor did when she was fed up, or scream and get hysterical like Kara, or just burst into tears and run away like Emily.

She was at 214 when her mother stood up. "I think that's the plane," Mrs. Sanchez said, pointing out the big glass windows.

Jo jumped out of her seat. "Come on, let's go!"

They hurried down the airport hallway to the doorway where the plane's passengers would come out. It seemed as if another hour passed before people finally started coming through the door. Finally a smiling flight attendant walked through beside a slim, tanned girl carrying a bright pink duffel bag. The girl's hair was dark brown like Jo's, but it was wavy instead of straight. Even though she hadn't seen her cousin for ages, Jo recognized her right away.

"Ceci!" Jo cried, hurrying forward.

The girl dropped her duffel bag. "Jo!" she shrieked, leaping forward. She grabbed Jo in a tight hug and spun her around and around.

"Stop!" Jo exclaimed, laughing. "I'm getting dizzy!"

Jo's parents were thanking the flight

attendant who had watched Ceci during
the flight. Ceci let go of Jo and rushed
over to give the flight attendant a hug.

"Thanks for being my travel buddy,"
Ceci said.

The flight attendant hugged her back
with a smile. "It was my pleasure, Ceci,"

she said. "Have a nice visit with your family."

The flight attendant hurried off with one last wave. Then Dr. and Mrs. Sanchez stepped forward to greet Ceci.

"*Hola*, Ceci," Mrs. Sanchez said, giving her niece a big hug. That was Spanish for "hello." Jo's whole family spoke Spanish as well as English. "We're so glad you could come."

"Me too. We're going to have a groovy time, aren't we, Jo?" Ceci giggled and tossed her hair out of her eyes. "That's my new favorite word," she explained. "Groovy. It means 'cool.'"

"We'll definitely have a groovy time." Jo grinned at her cousin. "I have your visit all planned out."

Ceci laughed. "I knew you would!" she said with a twinkle in her brown eyes. "You've always been a good planner."

Dr. Sanchez chuckled as he picked up

Ceci's duffel bag and slung it over his shoulder. "Did she tell you she arranged for you to go to school with her one day this week?"

Ceci's eyes widened. "Oh, no!" she cried, clutching her heart in mock horror. "I thought I escaped from having to go to school by coming here!"

"Quit it." Jo giggled and gave her a playful shove. "You already said in your e-mails that you couldn't wait to see my school. Anyway, you're coming with me on Tuesday. That's only two days before Thanksgiving, so we probably won't have to do much work, anyway."

"That's right." Mrs. Sanchez put an arm around Ceci's shoulders and steered her toward the exit. "On Monday while Jo is in school, you and I are going over to visit Grandpapa Sanchez. He can't wait to meet you."

"Groovy," Ceci said. "I can't wait to meet him, either."

Jo's grandfather lived in a town about ten miles from her own. He was her father's father. That meant he wasn't actually related to Ceci at all, since she was on Jo's mother's side of the family. But Grandpapa Sanchez said that anyone who was part of his grandchildren's family was part of his, too, even if they weren't blood relatives.

"So will I meet the rest of the Sleepover Squad on Tuesday?" Ceci asked Jo as they walked out of the airport. "Brr!" she cried without waiting for an answer. "It's freezing!"

Dr. Sanchez chuckled. "I forgot, you don't really have autumn in California, do you?"

"Sure we do." Ceci wrapped her arms around herself. "It's just a lot warmer there, that's all!"

Jo laughed along with her parents. "I have an extra jacket in the car you can borrow," she said. "Oh! And to answer your question, I hope you'll get to meet my friends a lot sooner than Tuesday. We were supposed to go see them right now, but we can't since your plane was so late. But they can't wait to meet you. I told you about the sleepover on Friday, right? We're all going to have so much fun together!"

"Yeah," Ceci agreed cheerfully. "But even better, you and I are going to have our own weeklong sleepover!"

Jo realized she was right. Ceci was going to sleep on a cot in her bedroom. Having her there all week would be kind of like an extra-long sleepover.

"That's true," Jo agreed. "It's going to be—"

Ceci didn't wait for her to finish. "Groovy!" she cried.

* 4 *

A Weeklong Sleepover

On Saturday night, Jo and Ceci talked until far into the night. Even though they had kept up with each other's lives through e-mails and phone calls, that wasn't the same as being together in person. There were a ton of things to talk about.

It was a little before eleven o'clock when Ceci yawned three times in a row.

"Are you getting sleepy?" Jo asked her cousin.

"No way. It's still early in California, remember?"

Jo nodded. She'd almost forgotten that Ceci's home was in a different time zone than her own.

But then she saw Ceci yawn again. "Uh-oh," Jo teased. "You'll have to stay awake later than this at the sleepover on Friday. We always stay up talking for half the night."

Ceci laughed. "Don't worry, I can stay up all night if I have to," she said. "I just need to rest my eyes for a second."

Jo watched as Ceci put her head down on her pillow. Less than a minute later she was snoring softly.

She's probably pretty tired from traveling all day to get here, Jo thought.

Jo was tired too. But her mind was racing as she thought about all the things she wanted to do tomorrow. It took her a few more minutes to fall asleep.

❊ ❊ ❊

The next morning, Jo and Ceci woke up to the scent of pancakes. When they went downstairs, breakfast was on the table.

"Hurry up and eat, girls," Mrs. Sanchez said. "We don't want to be late for church."

"You'll get to hear me sing in the choir," Jo told her cousin.

Ceci was already helping herself to the syrup. "Groovy," she said. "You've always been an awesome singer, Jo."

After church, they went home and changed clothes. Then Jo checked her watch. "We still have almost three hours before it's time for Taylor's soccer game to start," she said. "What do you want to do until then? We can either go into town and I can give you a tour, or we can go to the tennis club and play." Jo already knew that her cousin liked tennis almost as much as she did.

"Why can't we do both?" Ceci said.

Jo looked over at her father. "Is that okay?" she asked.

"Your wish is my command," Dr. Sanchez replied with a wink. He sometimes had to work at his medical practice on weekends, but he had taken the day off and promised to take Jo and Ceci wherever they wanted to go. "Let's hit the club first for a few games, and then I'll run you into town after that," he added. "Go grab your raquets and I'll meet you at the car."

As the fuzzy yellow ball sailed past her, Ceci collapsed on the court. "I give up!" she cried, waving her tennis raquet over her head. "You win—again. And now I'm starving. Any chance we could get a snack?"

"I know the perfect place," Jo said, hurrying around the net toward her cousin. "I'll ask Dad if he'll take us to my favorite ice-cream parlor." She grinned. "You're not too cold to eat ice cream, are you?"

"No way." Ceci sat up immediately. "Playing tennis warmed me up. Besides, it's never too cold for ice cream. Let's go!"

About forty minutes later they were standing in front of the counter at the ice-cream parlor. On the way there, Dr. Sanchez had driven all around town so

Jo could give Ceci a mini tour. They had even driven past Oak Tree Elementary. The school looked still and empty, as it always did on weekends.

"Check it out," Ceci cried, pointing up at the sign over the counter listing all the flavors. "They have coconut. That's my favorite!"

Jo nodded. The ice-cream parlor always had at least a dozen flavors to choose from, and they changed a lot. She liked to look into each of the vats behind the counter before she decided what flavor she wanted that day.

Jo was having a great time with her cousin. Ceci was just as lively and full of fun as she had remembered. When Jo was with her, she kind of forgot that she herself was usually more serious and practical. She just went along with Ceci and had fun without thinking too hard about anything else. It was kind of nice.

"What would you girls like?" Dr. Sanchez asked.

"Ooh, look at that!" Ceci pointed to something on the sign over the counter, then looked up at Dr. Sanchez. "Can we get the Belly Buster banana split?" she asked. "That's sounds super groovy!"

Dr. Sanchez raised an eyebrow. "Hmm, I don't know," he said. "That's meant for four people to share, and there are only three of us."

"It's okay." Ceci rubbed her stomach. "I'm hungry enough for two people."

Jo held her breath. Her parents had never let her order the Belly Buster before. But finally her father nodded.

"All right," he said, reaching for his wallet. "Let's go for it. But we can't leave until we've finished every bite, okay?"

"Deal!" Ceci said with a grin.

It took them a long time to finish the sundae. That was partly because it was very, very large. But it also took them a long time because they were so busy talking. First Jo and Ceci told Dr. Sanchez about their tennis matches. They had played several games, and Jo had won all except one. Luckily, Ceci didn't seem to mind that at all. She was a good sport.

Then Ceci told them all about her life in California. She was full of all kinds of funny stories about the people and places out there. She kept Jo and her father laughing so hard that they could hardly eat.

Finally, just as Ceci scooped up the last bite of hot fudge, Dr. Sanchez checked his watch. "It's getting late," he said. "We should head home before Anna wonders what happened to us."

Jo glanced out the ice-cream parlor's big plate-glass window. It was already starting to get dark outside. She blinked, wondering why that made her feel anxious.

Then, suddenly, she gasped. "Oh, no!" she cried, dropping her spoon with a clatter. "We forgot all about Taylor's soccer game!"

She couldn't believe it. She'd planned this whole day around cheering Taylor on at her big championship! That was also when Ceci was finally supposed to meet the rest of the Sleepover Squad.

"Oops." Dr. Sanchez shrugged. "You're right, *mi cara*. Sorry about that—I should have helped you remember."

"No." Jo shook her head. "It's my fault. I can't believe I forgot. Do you think we can hurry over there now? Maybe they're not finished yet."

Her father stood up and patted her on the head. "Sorry, Jo," he said. "That game is probably long over by now."

5

Members Only?

Jo felt terrible about missing Taylor's game. It was the biggest one of the whole season. How could she have forgotten something so important?

"Don't worry," Ceci told her as they left the ice-cream parlor and headed for the car. "Taylor is one of your best friends, right? She'll totally forgive you if you just explain what happened."

"You're right. After all, it's not every

day my favorite cousin comes to visit." Jo opened the car door and climbed in. "Still, I wish we'd remembered to go to the game."

"Me too." Ceci burped. "Oops! Excuse me. Um, I hope Aunt Anna doesn't mind if I don't eat any dinner tonight. After all that ice cream, I might not even be able to eat by Thanksgiving!"

Jo giggled. She was still worried about missing Taylor's game, but being with Ceci made her feel better. It was almost impossible to stay anxious or upset with her cousin around!

"Taylor!" Jo rushed up to her friends in their usual spot outside of homeroom the next day. "I'm so sorry I missed your game yesterday!"

"Yeah, what happened to you?" Kara frowned at her, looking confused. "Em and I saved seats for you and your cousin."

Emily nodded. She blinked at Jo, looking worried. "What happened? Did your dad's car break down?"

"No, nothing like that," Jo told her. Then she turned to Taylor. "But, anyway, I'm really sorry, Taylor. Will you forgive me?"

"Sure." Taylor shrugged. "It's not that big a deal."

"We were really looking forward to the game. Ceci likes sports, and she was ready to help cheer you on," Jo said. She dropped her backpack by her feet and leaned back against the wall. "I guess we just lost track of time. See, first we went to the tennis club and played for a while. Then we were hungry, so we went for ice cream." She giggled. "Ceci actually talked my dad into getting us the Belly Buster sundae, can you believe it? We finished the whole thing too! The only things left in the bowl were a little bit of caramel sauce and some walnuts. None of us likes walnuts very much."

Her friends didn't say anything for a moment. They all traded a glance. Taylor looked surprised. Emily looked anxious. Kara was starting to look annoyed.

"Hey," Kara said to Jo. "Aren't you even going to ask whether Taylor's team won the game?"

Jo felt her face turn red. "Oops," she said. "Um, I was just about to. So did you win, Taylor?"

"Uh-huh. Seven to four." Taylor shrugged. "It was pretty cool."

"Taylor scored three of the goals," Emily put in with a proud smile.

But Kara was still frowning. "So are you going to forget about all of us the whole time your cousin is visiting, Jo?" she complained.

"Sorry." Jo felt guilty. She hadn't meant to make any of her friends feel bad. "It's just that I haven't seen Ceci for so long, and she's so much fun. You guys will see that when you meet her tomorrow. Oh, and at the sleepover, of course."

"The sleepover?" Kara blinked. "What do you mean?"

Jo stared at her. "What do you mean, what do I mean?" she asked. "I mean we can all hang out at the sleepover and you guys can get to know Ceci better then. What do you think I mean?"

"Um . . ." Kara's voice trailed off.

All three of Jo's friends exchanged another look. Jo's eyes widened as she realized the truth.

"Wait," she said. "You guys knew Ceci would be around for our sleepover, right? I just thought . . ."

Her voice trailed off as Kara bit her lip. "I don't know," Kara said. "I guess I didn't really think about that. I was thinking it would be just the four of us, like usual."

"But it's no big deal—right, Kara?" Emily put in quickly. "The more the merrier."

Kara shrugged. "I don't know," she said again. "My parents might not let me invite another person."

Jo's eyes widened. "But I'm sure they'll understand—Ceci *has* to come—" she exclaimed. "Right, guys?" She looked at Emily and Taylor.

Emily nodded right away. But Taylor's greenish-gold eyes were troubled. "I don't know," she said. "I mean, having a new person there could be fun. But we've never had anyone except us at one of our sleepovers before."

"That's true," Kara said. "It would be weird to have a stranger there with us."

"But Ceci's not a stranger," Jo argued. "She's my cousin!"

"It'll be fine," Emily said with a little quiver in her voice. She hated when her friends fought. "We'll have fun with Ceci. Maybe I can bring my family's croquet set. You just said she likes sports, right, Jo?" She smiled hopefully. "We could even change the theme to be about California or something so she feels at home."

"Change the theme?" Taylor looked startled.

Kara crossed her arms over her chest, looking stubborn. "No way are we changing the theme," she said. "My mom already ordered the soccer ball cake. And we're going to have leftover Thanksgiving turkey sandwiches for dinner."

"Maybe we could make it a triple theme, then," Emily said in a small voice.

"Never mind, Em." Jo's surprise had passed. Now she was starting to feel angry. How could her friends even think about leaving Ceci out of the sleepover? "If you guys can't make room for Ceci, maybe you don't want me there either."

The bell rang before any of the others could answer, calling them all into homeroom. Jo stomped in ahead of the others, fuming. She couldn't believe they were being so stupid about this! For the rest of homeroom she didn't look at any of her friends. She just stared straight ahead at the blackboard.

Suddenly one of the best weeks of her life was turning into one of the worst!

6

What Now?

Jo was still feeling upset when she got home that afternoon. There had been a Thanksgiving assembly at lunch, which meant she hadn't had a chance to make up with her friends. That was okay with her. She wasn't even sure she *wanted* to make up with them. She could hardly believe how they were acting.

Okay, I know I shouldn't have forgotten about that soccer game, she told herself as she sat in the assembly. *But that wasn't Ceci's fault at all; it was mine. So why are Taylor and Kara taking it out on her by saying she can't come to the sleepover? I thought they were nicer than that.*

She thought about it all day. But she just couldn't make her friends' behavior make sense. They weren't being fair at all!

When the final bell rang, Jo rushed out of class as quickly as she could. Emily called after her, but Jo didn't slow down. She just called back that she was afraid of missing her bus. Then she ran off even faster.

After the bus dropped her off on Larkspur Lane, she walked into the house and hung her backpack on its hook in the front closet. Then she headed to the kitchen. Her mother and Ceci were in there making pies.

"*Hola,* Jo," Ceci said cheerfully. "How was school?"

"Oh, you know—it was school." Jo forced herself to smile. She didn't want Ceci to know what had happened. There was no sense in both of them feeling bad. "How was your visit with Grandpapa Sanchez?"

Ceci's face lit up. "It was great!" she exclaimed. "He has all kinds of really amazing stories. Did you know he once helped save, like, a hundred people after

an earthquake? He rode in on his best mustang horse and carried them all out to safety. Later on, the president of Mexico gave him a medal, but he doesn't have it anymore because he gave it to this little kid who was one of the people he rescued to cheer him up in the hospital."

"Uh-huh. He always has good stories like that."

"Yes." Mrs. Sanchez was rolling out some dough. She looked up with a smile. "Some of them are even true."

"Well, *I* totally believed every word!" Ceci grinned. "I told him I wished he was my *real* grandpa, and he said being a grandpa is a state of mind." She shrugged. "So then I started calling him my groovy grandpa, and he wasn't sure what I meant until I translated it into Spanish. Then he was happy."

"That's good." Jo was glad that Ceci and Grandpapa Sanchez had gotten along so well. That gave her an idea. "Hey," she said to her mother. "Since you guys had such a good time with Grandpapa, why don't we go to his house for the day after Thanksgiving? We can take the leftovers and have a picnic on his glassed-in porch."

Her mother looked surprised. "That's a nice thought, honey. But your Grandpapa is coming here for Thanksgiving dinner, remember? And then on Saturday he's riding along when your father drives your brother back to his college. So he'll probably want to rest on Friday."

"Oh." Jo had forgotten about all that. She bit her lip. After the big misunderstanding with her friends, she wasn't feeling very excited anymore about the sleepover—or even about taking Ceci to school with her. "Um, well, since Thanksgiving is coming up so soon, maybe Ceci should help you with the grocery shopping tomorrow." She glanced at Ceci. "I mean, it won't be that exciting at school, anyway. It'll probably be really boring. You won't be missing anything interesting."

"No way," Ceci said right away, sneaking a piece of dough into her mouth. "I can't wait to check out Oak Tree Elementary after everything you've told me about it. Besides, I still haven't met the rest of the Sleepover Squad yet, remember?"

"Oh. Right," Jo said weakly.

Her mother finished rolling out the piecrust, and she and Ceci started talking about what kinds of pies they were going to make for Thanksgiving dinner. But Jo wasn't paying much attention. Her stomach was in knots, and she couldn't decide what to do. What if she took Ceci to school tomorrow and Ceci started asking the others all kinds of questions about the sleepover? Jo still wasn't sure whether her cousin was going to be invited or not.

Kara wouldn't really un-invite her right to her face, would she? Jo thought. *She's not that mean. Then again, she sometimes does blurt things out without thinking about it. She might not realize it if she was hurting Ceci's feelings. And Taylor seems a little unsure about the whole thing. . . .*

But she knew one thing for certain: She would never forgive herself if her stupid argument with her friends ended up making Ceci wish she'd never come to visit!

✳ 7 ✳

Season of Change

Is that them over there?" Ceci peered down the crowded school hallway. "I think I see them. I totally recognize them all from your descriptions! Kara's the red-headed one in the girly dress, Taylor's the tall, athletic one, and Emily is the pale, quiet-looking one with the long, straight blond hair."

"That's right," Jo said, trying not to let on how nervous she felt. She still hadn't figured out how to tell Ceci about her argument with the rest of the Sleepover Squad.

And now it was too late. Ceci was already hurrying forward with a big smile on her face.

"*Hola*, everyone!" she greeted Jo's friends cheerfully. "I'm Ceci."

"Wow, you totally are!" Kara exclaimed with a laugh. "I would've recognized you anywhere. You look just like Jo but with shorter hair!"

Ceci patted her hair and grinned. "Yeah, I thought about that," she said. "I could almost trade places with Jo and live here while she went to California to live with my family for a while, and nobody would even know. But then I found out it gets freezing cold here in the winter, and I changed my mind." She wrapped her arms around herself and pretended to shiver, even though it was warm in the hallway.

Emily giggled. "Just like the Prince and
the Pauper!"

Ceci looked confused. Taylor laughed.
"That's a book our teacher read us in class
last year about two boys switching places.
Leave it to Emmers to remember—in case
Jo didn't tell you, Em's book crazy! By the
way, I'm Taylor."

"I know. Jo told me all about you."
Ceci grinned at her. "She said you're the

world's greatest soccer player. And you"—she turned and pointed at Kara—"You're Kara, and you love to laugh and hate getting dirty. And Emily loves animals—especially horses."

"You really *could* switch places with Jo," Emily exclaimed. "You already know all about her life!"

"But did Jo warn you that I have four rotten, obnoxious brothers?" Kara asked Ceci. "Or did she keep it a secret so you wouldn't be too scared to come to the sleepover on Friday?"

Jo blinked, hardly believing her ears. Was she imagining it? Or had Kara just pretty much invited Ceci to the sleepover herself?

"Oh, she told me about them, all right," Ceci was saying with a grin. "But don't worry. My other cousins—the ones on my mom's side, not my dad's like Jo—are three of the most obnoxious boys in the entire universe. And they live right down the street from me. If I can handle *them*, your brothers won't stand a chance!"

Kara, Taylor, and Emily all laughed at that. Jo laughed too—mostly with relief. She should have known her friends wouldn't be mean to Ceci. They just weren't that way. It was one of the reasons they were her friends.

After that, Jo's friends and Ceci chattered nonstop, laughing and getting to know one another better. But Jo hardly heard any of it. She was too busy trying to figure out what had just happened.

I don't get it, she thought as she watched the others. *My friends are getting along great with Ceci, just like I knew they would. So then why were they so weird about her yesterday?*

"I'm going to get another chocolate milk." Ceci hopped up from her seat.

"Anyone want anything while I'm up there?"

"No, thanks," Jo replied. Her friends shook their heads.

Ceci got up and hurried across the cafeteria. It was lunchtime, and the Sleepover Squad girls were at their usual table near the windows.

As soon as Ceci was out of earshot, Taylor leaned toward Jo with a serious look on her face. "Listen, Jo-Jo," she said. "I didn't want to say anything while Ceci was around. But I'm totally sorry about our stupid fight yesterday."

"Me too," Kara put in, looking up from her sandwich. "You just took me by surprise, that's all. I hadn't really thought about how if Ceci was visiting you all week, that meant she would be coming to the sleepover with you too."

Taylor nodded. "Yeah," she said. "It was kind of weird to think about the Sleepover

Squad ever changing, you know?"

"Thanks, guys. I'm sorry too." Jo was so relieved, she could hardly stand it. "I guess I was so distracted by Ceci's visit that I forgot about everything else, including Taylor's big game. That was just as wrong as anything you guys did."

"Cool! Then we're even." Taylor smiled. "And now that I've met Ceci, I can see that having her at the sleepover is going to be a *good* change. She's awesome!"

Jo smiled as the others agreed with Taylor. She was glad that her friends liked Ceci as much as she did.

"If you think about it, an autumn sleepover is the perfect time for a change," Emily said. "After all, autumn is the season of change. The weather changes from warm summer to cold winter, the leaves change colors. . . ."

Before any of the others could respond, a mustard-covered slice of bologna landed on the table right in front of Jo with a *splat*. "Hey!" Jo cried in surprise. She spun around in her seat to see where it had come from.

Randy Blevins and Max Wolfe were grinning at her from the next table. "Oops!" Max called. "Sorry, Jo. We were actually aiming at Taylor's head."

"Yeah," Randy added. "I don't know how we missed such a big target."

Taylor let out a yell, then jumped out of her seat and rushed toward the boys. Jo giggled as she watched her friend grab a slice of mustardy bread and wipe it on Randy's face.

"Oh well," Jo said to Kara and Emily. "I guess some things never change!"

8

Trying Too Hard

The rest of the week seemed to fly by. Thanksgiving at Jo's house was busy, crowded, and lots of fun. Her older sister, Lydia, and older brother, Alfonso, came home from their colleges. Grandpapa Sanchez rode over with Jo's aunt, uncle, and cousins, who lived in the same town as he did. All of them gathered in the dining room with Jo, her parents, and Ceci. There were so many people that Jo's father had to put two extra leaves in the dining room table. They chatted in English and Spanish, joked around and laughed until their sides hurt, and of course ate a lot. They had a big, juicy turkey with Mrs. Sanchez's special corn bread stuffing flavored with chorizo and jalapeño peppers. There was also cranberry sauce, mashed plantains, two types of salad, several vegetables, and three kinds of pie.

Over dessert, Grandpapa Sanchez told a long, funny story about how he'd run away to Cuba when he was a teenager and supported himself by giving dance lessons to tourists. When a couple of the adults didn't believe him, he told them he'd prove it. He got up and, even with his bad leg, taught the younger kids how to dance the mambo! Jo ended up giggling so hard, she could hardly stand, let alone dance.

Later, she and Ceci stayed up until midnight talking with the relatives. When they finally fell into bed, they fell asleep right away. Normally Jo's parents didn't like anyone to sleep too late, but on Friday morning they didn't wake the girls up until after ten o'clock.

Jo's sister, Lydia, smiled as Jo and Ceci came into the kitchen for breakfast, still yawning. "We thought you sleepyheads would be in bed all day," she teased.

"Yeah," Jo's brother, Al, said from over near the sink. "You slept long enough to get out of doing the dishes. We just finished them all."

Ceci giggled. "That was our plan!"

She was only kidding, though. After breakfast, Ceci and Jo helped clean up the house until it was time to leave for the sleepover. Then Al drove them to Kara's house. She lived in a brick house in the middle of town, just a few blocks away from Taylor's family.

"Come on in!" Kara exclaimed, throwing the door open as soon as they knocked. Her Labrador retriever, Chester, was there too. He barked and wagged his tail happily. "Taylor and Em are already here," Kara went on. "But don't worry, we waited for you guys to start watching the movies Mom rented for us."

Jo stepped inside, suddenly feeling a little bit anxious. In all the excitement of the holiday, she'd sort of forgotten about how Ceci would be the first-ever outside guest at a Sleepover Squad slumber party. But now she remembered all over again. Would having Ceci there make the sleepover feel different? And if it did, would her friends be upset about it? She hoped not. She was going to do everything she could to make sure that everyone had a good time.

"Aw, what a cute dog!" Ceci bent down to pet Chester. "I wish I could have a dog. But my dad's allergic."

"Oh, right," Jo said. "Hey Kara, that reminds me. Did I remember to tell you that Ceci is allergic to shellfish?"

"You told me," Kara said with a laugh. "Twice, I think. And don't worry, I'm pretty sure there's no shellfish in leftover turkey. Or in soccer-shaped cakes, either."

Ceci nodded. "Yeah, don't worry, Jo. I heard you tell her about my allergy at school the other day. So everything's groovy." She dropped her duffel and the sleeping bag she'd borrowed from Jo, then looked around. "This is such a cute house, Kara!"

"Thanks." Kara shrugged. "Mom says it has that lived-in look. I think she means there's dog hair everywhere and my brothers never pick up after themselves. Come on, I'll give you a tour!"

Jo had seen Kara's house lots of times. But she trailed along as Kara showed Ceci around, with Chester trotting along after them. They walked through the first floor to the comfortably cluttered kitchen, where they said hello to Kara's parents. Then they went up to the second floor.

"You probably don't want to see inside my brothers' rooms." Kara pointed to two doors. One was cracked open a little bit, and the sound of loud rock music poured out of it. The other was shut and had a KEEP OUT! sign on it. Jo knew that the first door led into the room shared by Kara's older brothers, Chip and Eddie. The other one belonged to their two younger brothers Mark and Todd. "Not unless you want to be scared, anyway," Kara added with a shudder.

"Well, I like to be scared sometimes," Ceci replied with a grin. "That reminds

me, did you get any horror movies for us to watch tonight? I love scary movies!"

"No way," Jo spoke up before Kara could answer. She didn't want Kara to think that Ceci might be complaining about their movie selections. "Emily gets too scared by horror movies. We *never* watch them at our sleepovers."

"Oh." Ceci shrugged. "That's cool. So what are we seeing?"

Kara told her the names of the movies. Then they walked down the hall and up the narrow staircase to the third floor. Since Kara was the only girl in the family, she was also the only one with her own bedroom. It was a tiny, cozy space next to the attic. When they reached the landing, the door was open. Taylor and Emily were inside Kara's room laying out their sleeping bags.

"Hi, guys!" Emily looked up, brushed her hair out of her face, and smiled. "Happy Thanksgiving!"

"Yeah, same here." Taylor hopped to her feet. "I'm glad you guys finally got here. Let's get downstairs and start making popcorn for the movies!"

"Groovy." Ceci led the way back down the steps. "How do you guys make your popcorn? Back home, I usually make it with Cajun seasoning."

"We don't do that," Jo said quickly. "We *always* make it with just butter and salt." She definitely didn't want the other members of the Sleepover Squad to think that Ceci was trying to boss them into making popcorn a different way!

"Yeah, I don't think we have any Cajun seasoning," Kara said. She licked her lips. "But it sounds yummy. We'll have to try that sometime, right guys?"

Taylor laughed. "You think everything sounds yummy, Kara," she teased. "You'd probably eat popcorn with fried clams and squid on it!"

"But not tonight, right?" Jo put in. "Ceci's allergic to shellfish. She breaks out in hives if she even smells clams or shrimp or lobster or anything like that."

Ceci shot her a strange look. "Yeah, you already told them that, remember?"

"Oh." For a second, Jo felt kind of silly for repeating herself. But she shrugged if off. After all, she was the only one who knew everyone at the party very well. She wanted to make sure there were no misunderstandings like the one she'd had with her friends earlier in the week. Otherwise the sleepover could turn into a disaster.

When they got back downstairs, Kara's six-year-old twin brothers were sitting on the couch in the front room. They were watching cartoons on TV.

"Hi there, Carrot-top Twins," Taylor greeted them. That was her favorite nickname for the boys. They both had red hair the same shade as Kara's.

Kara frowned at them. "What are you two doing in here?" she demanded. "Mom and Dad said we get to use the TV to watch our movies."

"Aw, come on," Mark whined. "Can't we just watch the end of this show?"

"No way." Kara crossed her arms over her chest. "Get out."

Todd jumped to his feet. "You'll be sorry," he said with a mischievous grin. "We shall have our revenge!"

"Ha ha ha ha ha!" Mark bellowed in a monster-movie voice.

Kara just rolled her eyes as the twins scooted off toward the basement door. But Jo bit her lip, feeling worried. What if the boys really did try to get revenge by playing practical jokes on them? Jo wasn't sure what Ceci would think if she found her duffel bag stuffed full of worms or one of the boys' pet lizards under her pillow.

Jo was so nervous about what the boys might do that she couldn't really concentrate on the movie. Halfway through, they paused the DVD so Taylor could go to the bathroom. Meanwhile, Emily looked over at Jo.

"Are you okay, Jo?" Emily asked. "You aren't laughing at the funny parts."

"I'm fine," Jo replied quickly. "Everything

is totally fine. This sleepover is fun, isn't it? Just like all the others."

"Uh-huh." Kara gave her a strange look. "I guess."

Just then Taylor came back. Jo leaned back on the couch, trying to act normal. But she still felt tense. Every time Ceci laughed more loudly than the others or shouted "Groovy!" at something, it reminded Jo that having her cousin there was different. Were her friends thinking the same thing?

What if they get tired of her and wish she hadn't come? she wondered. *Or what if the boys play a prank on her just because she's new? That kind of sounds like something they'd do. . . .*

She was still worrying when the movie ended. Ceci got up and looked out the window. "Want to go outside and play hide and seek or something?" she suggested. "We still have time before dinner, right?"

"Are you sure?" Taylor asked with a grin. "I thought it would be too cold for you out there, California Girl."

Jo shot her a look. Was she just joking around? Or did she really think Ceci was a weather wimp?

Before she could figure it out, Ceci laughed. "I'm getting used to it," she told Taylor. "But if you guys are too scared to play against the best hide-and-seeker in California—"

"Let's go." Taylor headed for the front door. "And get ready to watch a *real* hide-and-seek champion in action!"

They played outside for about an hour. When it started to get dark, they headed back in. All four of Kara's brothers were in the front room this time.

"Hi, you guys," Kara said. "What's up?"

Jo was a little surprised. Kara hardly ever acted friendly toward her brothers, especially during sleepovers. But she was glad. The less Kara fought with her brothers tonight, the less chance they would play one of their pranks.

"Not much," answered Chip, the oldest brother. "Oh, but Mom wants one of you to go down in the basement and bring up an extra chair for Ceci to sit in at dinner."

"I'll go," Jo offered. She hurried toward the basement door and opened it.

S P L A S H !
Jo gasped as a giant water balloon fell right on her head and burst. She was soaked!

9

Pranks and Pen Pals

"Hey!" Jo shouted in surprise.

The sound of laughter came from behind her. Spinning around, she saw the boys laughing hard. That was no surprise. The water balloon was exactly the kind of prank they loved to pull.

But then Jo heard more laughter. Taylor was giggling. Emily and Kara were grinning at each other.

Now Jo was surprised. If it had been only the boys who had played this joke, there was no way Kara would be laughing. She would be yelling at them. And the others would be backing her up.

Jo was a logical person. It didn't take her long to realize what this meant. "No way!" she cried, glaring at her friends. "Did you guys actually know about this? Were you in on it with the boys? How could you do something like this?"

"Whoa, whoa!" Taylor stopped laughing and held up both her hands. "Hang on a second, Jo-Jo. Let us explain."

"What is there to explain?" Jo couldn't remember the last time she'd been so angry. All the anxiety of the last few days poured out of her at once. "What if it had been Ceci who'd got drenched just now, huh?" She shook her head, sending water flying in every direction. "What would she think of us then? Are you trying to chase her off because she's not an official member of the Sleepover Squad or something?"

"Huh?" Kara looked startled. "No, that's not it at all!"

"She's right." Ceci stepped forward. She had been laughing too. But now she looked serious. "Anyway, it couldn't have been me who got drenched, Jo. See, this whole prank was *my* idea."

"Yeah," Chip put in. "You can't blame us for this one."

Eddie nodded. "We just supplied the water balloon . . . um . . . and helped set it up. But it was all Ceci's idea. She sneaked in during your hide-and-seek game to tell us what to do."

"Huh?" Jo blinked at her cousin, not understanding.

"I'm super sorry, Jo." Ceci grabbed Jo's wet hands and squeezed them. "I thought it would be funny. And you've always told me how Kara's brothers love practical jokes. Anyway, I didn't know you'd get so upset or I never would have done it."

But all of a sudden Jo wasn't upset anymore. At least, she wasn't upset with Ceci, or the rest of the Sleepover Squad, or even with Kara's brothers. The only one she was a little bit upset with was herself.

"No, *I'm* sorry," she told Ceci. "I just realized something. You guys are all getting along fine."

Kara looked confused. "What, do you mean me and my brothers are getting along?" She shot the boys a slightly suspicious look. "Don't count on that lasting."

Jo laughed and shook her head. "I mean you guys and Ceci," she explained. "You're all having a great time together at this sleepover."

"Of course we are, Jo-Jo." Taylor shrugged. "Why wouldn't we? Ceci's cool."

"Don't you mean 'groovy'?" Emily corrected with a giggle.

Everyone laughed, including Ceci. Jo was relieved. This time she didn't even have to wonder if Emily was joking around. She knew she was teasing Ceci the same way all the members of the Sleepover Squad teased one another sometimes. Like *friends*.

"Never mind," Jo said. "Come on, let's get back to our sleepover!"

Todd ran and got a towel so Jo could dry herself off. Then the boys wandered off while the girls all returned to the front room. As the others argued about whether to start another DVD before dinner or wait until later, Jo just sat back and watched with a smile.

Ceci practically seems like an honorary member of the Sleepover Squad already, she thought. *I think the others realized that before I did. But now that I've figured it out, maybe I can finally relax and start having fun at this sleepover!*

Kara yawned. "What time is it?" she mumbled sleepily, resting her chin on her arms.

"Almost midnight," Taylor told her. Then she looked over at Ceci, who was sitting cross-legged on her sleeping bag on Kara's bedroom floor. "Kara's almost always the first one to fall asleep at all our sleepovers," Taylor told her. "Usually that means we play some kind of prank on her."

"Remember our very first sleepover?" Emily said. "We were going to stick that leftover cupcake to Kara's forehead when she fell asleep."

Jo giggled, remembering that night. "But when we tried, she grabbed it and ate it!" she finished the story.

Ceci laughed. "That's funny," she said. "This sleepover is great, you guys! I think I'm going to get my friends back home to start having them. Maybe we can even start up our own California chapter of the Sleepover Squad. What do you think?"

"Groovy!" Kara said, sitting up and looking a little more awake. "You should definitely do that, Ceci."

Emily nodded. "Then you can write to us and e-mail pictures of your parties and stuff, and we can write back to you the same way," she suggested. "We can all be like sleepover pen pals or something."

"That's a great idea." Ceci looked excited. "Let's definitely do that!"

Jo glanced at her watch. "Three, two, one . . . it's midnight," she announced. "That means it's officially two days after Thanksgiving now."

Taylor climbed out of her sleeping bag. "That gives me a great idea," she said. "Who's hungry for a midnight snack of leftover turkey?"

"Me!" Now Kara looked totally awake.

"Me too," Emily agreed.

"Me three," Ceci said.

Jo smiled. "Me four. Let's go!"

They headed downstairs, tiptoeing so they wouldn't wake up Kara's family. Soon they were all sitting at the kitchen table eating cold leftover turkey.

"Happy two days after Thanksgiving, everyone," Emily said, popping a piece of white meat into her mouth. "What are you guys thankful for?"

"Oh, all kinds of stuff," Taylor said. "Like my team's soccer championship, and for all my friends, including the new ones. . . ." She turned to smile at Ceci.

Jo felt pretty thankful herself when she heard that. She was grateful for having such nice friends—and such an awesome cousin, too. She was also thankful that everyone seemed to agree that change could sometimes be a good thing.

"I've got one," Kara mumbled with her mouth full. "I'm thankful that my piggy brothers didn't eat the entire turkey yet."

Ceci laughed. "Well, I'm thankful for the

Sleepover Squad," she exclaimed. "You guys are the grooviest!"

Jo smiled. She knew they could all agree with that!

Slumber Party Project:
Far-Flung Friends

Jo's cousin Ceci had a great time hang-ing out with the Sleepover Squad during her visit. She's also looking for-ward to having a great time being pen pals with them. Just because someone lives far away doesn't mean she can't still be part of your life! In fact, why not have a Pen Pal Party for your next sleepover?

Tell everyone who's invited to bring the name and address of a distant friend or rela-tive to be their pen pal. Is there a friend from your school who has moved away? If so, maybe everyone can share the same pen pal.

Anyone can send a long-distance friend

an e-mail or an IM. So why not let your pen pal know she's something special by sending your messages the old-fashioned way? But don't just write an ordinary letter—get creative! At your sleepover, you and your friends can help one another come up with fun ideas to send to your pals. Draw pictures, write silly poems or coded letters or lists of your favorite and least favorite things, make up your own funny cartoons about your lives, cut pictures out of your favorite magazines and turn them into fun collages, print out digital photos of yourself and decorate them with glitter—anything you think your friend will like!

When you're finished, put the whole thing in an envelope and ask your parents to put a stamp on it and mail it for you. That way, your pen pal will have something special to keep that reminds her of you. And if you're lucky, maybe she'll send you something just as cool in return!